I Learn from My Uncle

Mary Austen

illustrated by
Anita Morra

PowerKiDS press.

New York

Published in 2018 by The Rosen Publishing Group, Inc.
29 East 21st Street, New York, NY 10010

First Edition

Managing Editor: Nathalie Beullens-Maoui
Editor: Greg Roza
Art Director: Michael Flynn
Book Design: Raúl Rodriguez
Illustrator: Anita Morra

Cataloging-in-Publication Data

Names: Austen, Mary.
Title: I learn from my uncle / Mary Austen.
Description: New York : PowerKids Press, 2018. | Series: The things I learn | Includes index.
Identifiers: ISBN 9781538327142 (pbk.) | ISBN 9781508163756 (library bound) | ISBN 9781538327821 (6 pack)
Subjects: LCSH: Social learning–Juvenile literature. | Uncles–Juvenile literature.
Classification: LCC HQ783 .A87 2018 | DDC 303.3'27—dc23

Manufactured in the United States of America

CPSIA Compliance Information: Batch #BW18PK. For further information contact Rosen Publishing, New York, New York at 1-800-237-9932

Contents

My uncle is so cool! He teaches me new things all the time.

5

My uncle likes sports.

He teaches me how to play baseball.

My uncle shows me how to use a bat.

I learn to throw
the ball too.

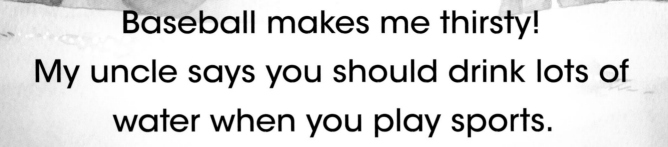

Baseball makes me thirsty!
My uncle says you should drink lots of
water when you play sports.

My uncle plays the piano.

He teaches me to play the piano too!

I like to sing.

My uncle teaches me the words
to a song.

He plays piano and I sing along.

My uncle shows me how to read his watch.

It's 5 o'clock.

It's time for dinner!

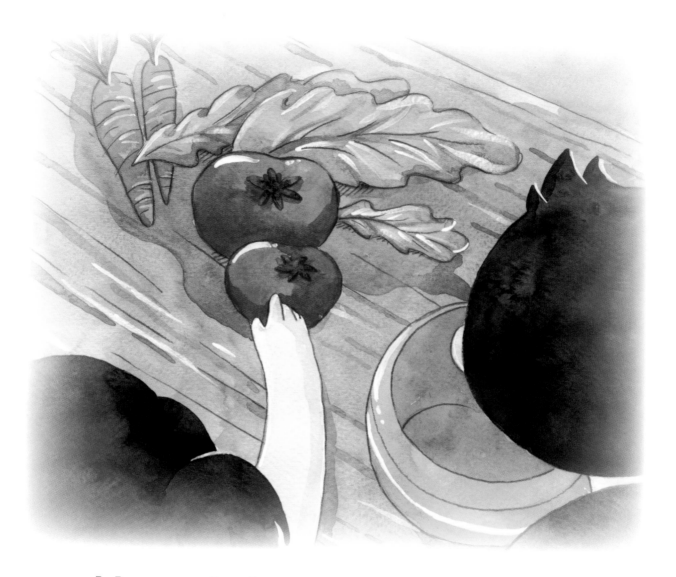

My uncle teaches me to make
a yummy salad.

Learning with my uncle is fun!

Words to Know

baseball

piano

watch

Index

B
baseball, 7, 11

D
dinner, 20

P
piano, 12, 13, 16

S
sports, 6, 11